April & Mae
and the
Tea Party

EVERY DAY
WITH
April & Mae

SUNDAY

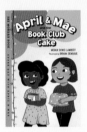

MONDAY

TUESDAY

WEDNESDAY

THURSDAY

FRIDAY

SATURDAY

Collect them ALL!

April & Mae

and the

Tea Party

THE SUNDAY BOOK

MEGAN DOWD LAMBERT

Illustrated by BRIANA DENGOUE

i◚i Charlesbridge

To Karen Boss, my extraordinary editor and
even better friend—M. D. L.

To my daughter, Bellarose—B. D.

Text copyright © 2022 by Megan Dowd Lambert
Illustrations copyright © 2022 by Briana Arrington-Dengoue
All rights reserved, including the right of reproduction in whole
or in part in any form. Charlesbridge and colophon are registered
trademarks of Charlesbridge Publishing, Inc.

At the time of publication, all URLs printed in this book were accurate
and active. Charlesbridge, the author, and the illustrator are not responsible
for the content or accessibility of any website.

Published by Charlesbridge
9 Galen Street, Watertown, MA 02472 • (617) 926-0329
www.charlesbridge.com

Library of Congress Cataloging-in-Publication Data
Names: Lambert, Megan Dowd, author. | Dengoue, Briana, illustrator.
Title: April & Mae and the tea party: the Sunday book / Megan Dowd Lambert;
    illustrated by Briana Dengoue.
Description: Watertown, MA: Charlesbridge, 2022. | Series: Every Day with
    April & Mae | Audience: Ages 5–8. | Summary: "April and Mae are best
    friends (and so are their pets). One day angry words are exchanged and they
    must find a way to apologize and save their friendship."—Provided
    by publisher.
Identifiers: LCCN 2019035078 (print) | LCCN 2019035079 (ebook) |
    ISBN 9781580898867 (hardback) | ISBN 9781632897503 (ebook)
Subjects: LCSH: Best friends—Juvenile fiction. | Friendship—Juvenile fiction. |
    Anger—Juvenile fiction. | Apologizing—Juvenile fiction. | CYAC:
    Best friends—Fiction. | Friendship—Fiction. | Pets—Fiction.
Classification: LCC PZ7.1.L26 Ap 2022 (print) | LCC PZ7.1.L26 (ebook) |
    DDC [E]—dc23
LC record available at https://lccn.loc.gov/2019035078
LC ebook record available at https://lccn.loc.gov/2019035079

Printed in China
(hc) 10 9 8 7 6 5 4 3 2 1

Illustrations done in Procreate
Display type set in Jacoby by Adobe
Text type set in Grenadine by Markanna Studios Inc.
Color separations and printing by 1010 Printing International Limited
    in Huizhou, Guangdong, China
Production supervision by Jennifer Most Delaney
Designed by Cathleen Schaad

April and Mae
are not the same.

April loves her dog.
Mae loves her cat.
Mae is tidy.
April is not.
April is showy.
Mae is not.

But April and Mae are friends.
Best friends.
And their pets
are best friends, too.

On Sundays,
April and Mae have tea.
Mae bakes goodies
and sets the table,
just so.

April sings and dances.
Mae claps and claps,
and April bows.

The pets play.
They all eat.
It is fun!

Then one Sunday,
Mae bakes goodies
and sets the table,
just so.

But April says,
"Today, I will not
sing or dance."
"No?" says Mae.
"No," says April.
"Today, I have a *new* act."
"Today, I want to *see* a new act,"
says Mae.

"Sit down, please," says April.
"And close your eyes
 until I say 'TA-DA!'"
Mae sits down
and closes her eyes.
April takes three balls
from her bag.
"*TA-DA!*" says April.

Mae opens her eyes.
April juggles the balls.
Mae opens her eyes wider.
April juggles the balls faster.

Then *BONK!*
One ball hits Mae's cat.
MEOW!

And *BOOP!*
One ball hits April's dog.
WOOF!

And *BANG!*
One ball hits Mae's table, just so.
CRASH!

"I am sorry!" says April.
"Let me try again."

"*NO!*" yells Mae.
"You are a bad juggler."

"That is not nice!" says April.
"I am a *new* juggler."

"It is not nice to break teacups,"
 says Mae.
"Just *one* teacup," says April.
"The *best* teacup," says Mae.
 Their pets
 are quiet and still.

"Just go," says Mae.
"But—" says April.
"GO!" yells Mae.

18

So April goes,
and her dog goes, too.

Now April and Mae
are the same.

They are sad.
They are mad.
They are lonely, too.

On Sunday,
they do not have tea.
Mae does not bake goodies
or set the table,
just so.

April does not sing
or dance
or juggle.
Mae does not clap.
April does not bow.
The pets do not play.
No one eats goodies.
It is not fun.

"Argh!" says Mae.
"That was the *best* teacup!"

"Ugh!" says April.
"I am a *new* juggler!"
And their pets
are quiet and still.

"Have a goody," says Mae.
But her cat
will not eat.

"Look at me!" says April.
But her dog
will not look.

April and Mae
are friends.
Best friends.
What can they do?

They do not
want to be mad.
They do not
want to be sad.
They do not want
their pets to feel blue.

Mae writes a note.

Dear April,
I am sorry I yelled.
You are brave
to try a new act.
Please come to tea.
Love, Mae

April reads the note
and cries happy tears.
"Boo-hoo!"

Then April
writes a note, too.

Dear Mae,
I am sorry I broke
your best teacup.
You are sweet
to make things
just so.
I will come to tea.
Love, April

But at tea on Sunday,
the pets play
and eat goodies,
and April and Mae just sit.

And sit.

And sit.

It is not fun.

Then April's dog
taps the box
by the table.

"Oh, yes!" says April.

 April gives the box to Mae.

"For me?" says Mae.

"Yes," says April.

"Please read the note."

Dear Mae,
A new teacup
for my best friend.
I am sorry.
Love, April

Now Mae cries
happy tears, too.
"Boo-hoo!"

Then Mae's cat
jumps on the table,
just so.
"Look," says Mae.
"A gift for you, too."
"Wow!" says April.
"Juggling scarves!"

"There is a note, too," says Mae.
April reads the note.

Dear April,
You are the best,
and I am sorry.
Love, Mae

It took time.
It took gifts and notes, too.
But April and Mae
are still friends.
Best friends.
And their pets
do not feel blue.

45

Mae gives out goodies.
April sings
and dances
and juggles.
Mae claps and claps,
and April bows.

The pets play.
They all eat.
It is fun!
It is the *best!*

It is a new start.

It is also . . .
The End.